Namaste!
I am Woka Chimni, an Indian house sparrow. I love my cozy home in Mumbai, masala chai and reading. But what I love most is exploring new places in my beautiful country, India.
Come join me on my exciting adventures!

Book 1

The Adventures of
WOKA CHIMNI

Written by
Preeti Vyas

· Illustrated and designed by
Happy Fish

PUFFIN BOOKS
An imprint of Penguin Random House

FUNOKPLEASE

FunOKPlease Content Publishing Pvt. Ltd
Pitamber Lane, Mahim
Mumbai 400016

In collaboration with

PUFFIN BOOKS

USA | Canada | UK | Ireland | Australia
New Zealand | India | South Africa | China

Puffin Books is part of the Penguin Random House group of companies
whose addresses can be found at global.penguinrandomhouse.com

Published by Penguin Random House India Pvt. Ltd
7th Floor, Infinity Tower C, DLF Cyber City,
Gurgaon 122 002, Haryana, India

First published in Puffin Books by Penguin Random House India 2018

ISBN 9780143442004

Printed at Parksons Graphics Pvt. Ltd, India

WOKA
IN THE
SUNDERBANS

Woka was sitting in her cozy armchair, sipping some delicious masala chai and enjoying the pitter-patter of raindrops outside. 'Oh, I just love the rain. Each little leaf gets a nice bath and starts sparkling afterwards,' she said to herself.

She walked towards her big bookshelf to get something to read, when she felt a tingling in her feet.

'Hmm, my feet are beginning to itch. I think it's time to travel again. Where should I go this time? Let me peek into my favourite book to decide ...

Ooh, the Sunderbans! Floating islands, rare trees, beautiful birds and exotic animals, including tigers—my favourite! *And* it's the largest mangrove forest in the world. Yes, that's where I will go!'

'It's time to pack everything I need: my backpack, my know-it-all assistant, GeePee, and my emergency snack box full of sweets and nuts. GeePee, how long will it take to reach the Sunderbans?'

- Backpack ✓
- GeePee ✓
- Snack pack ✓

Let's gooooo!

GeePee replied, 'Sunderbans. Flight time: 2 days.'

Mumbai

Nashik

Aurangabad

Nagpur

Raipur

Kolkata

Sunderbans

With GeePee's help, Woka flew towards the Sunderbans in West Bengal. She flew over the vineyards in Nashik and the Ajanta and Ellora caves in Aurangabad. She flew over the orange groves in Nagpur and the chimneys of the steel factories in Raipur. Finally, after a quick rest near Kolkata's Victoria Memorial, she arrived at the Sunderbans.

'Wow! This looks even better than the pictures in my book. Look at the beautiful floating mangroves! And so much wildlife: turtles, fishing cats, snakes, porcupines, wild boars and hundreds of red fiddler crabs. This is simply amazing.'

Suddenly, she heard a whimper. She looked down and saw the cutest little tiger cub, crying.

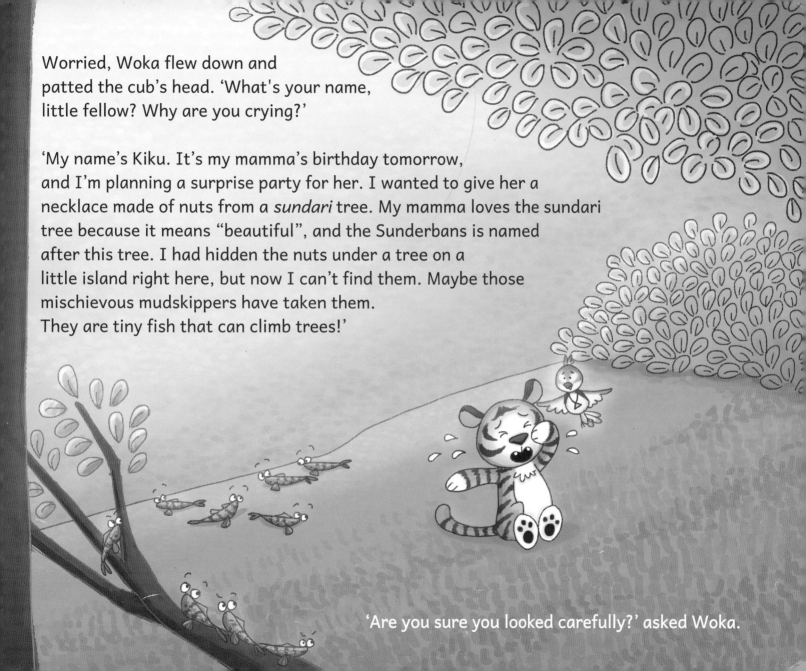

Worried, Woka flew down and patted the cub's head. 'What's your name, little fellow? Why are you crying?'

'My name's Kiku. It's my mamma's birthday tomorrow, and I'm planning a surprise party for her. I wanted to give her a necklace made of nuts from a *sundari* tree. My mamma loves the sundari tree because it means "beautiful", and the Sunderbans is named after this tree. I had hidden the nuts under a tree on a little island right here, but now I can't find them. Maybe those mischievous mudskippers have taken them. They are tiny fish that can climb trees!'

'Are you sure you looked carefully?' asked Woka.

SPLASH! A beautiful pink Gangetic dolphin suddenly swam up to them.
'Hey, I'm Gajli! Where are you from, little sparrow?
I've never seen you here before,' she asked Woka.

'I'm Woka Chimni from Mumbai, and I'm here to visit your beautiful home.

But right now, I'm worried about this little tiger cub.
He's lost his precious sundari nuts, which he'd hidden on
an island. Do you know what could have happened to them?'

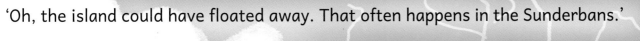

'Oh, the island could have floated away. That often happens in the Sunderbans.'

'Floated away?' Woka was surprised.

'Well, as you know, the Sunderbans is a giant floating forest with more than 100 islands. Whenever this region floods, little islands do float away. It's quite magical.'

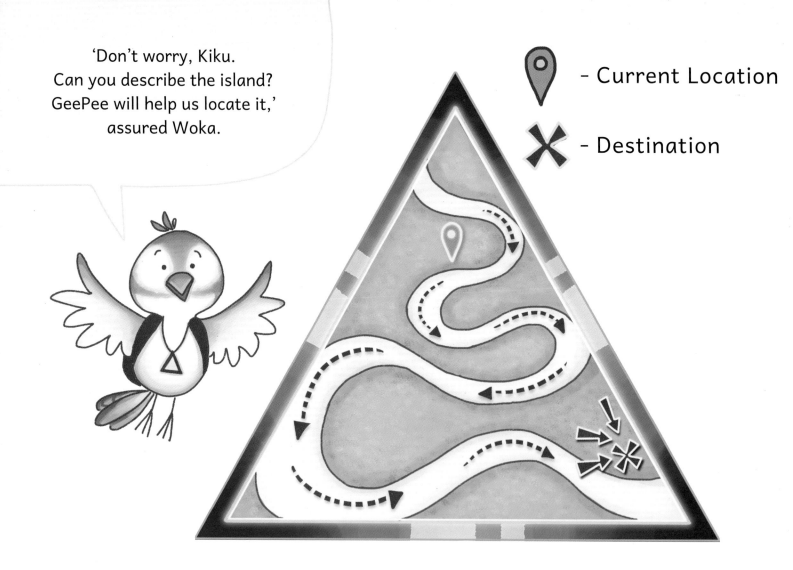

'Don't worry, Kiku.
Can you describe the island?
GeePee will help us locate it,'
assured Woka.

- Current Location

- Destination

Kiku told her all that he could remember about the island. GeePee sprang to attention, beeping and displaying a blinking arrow that pointed south.

'Oh, that's quite far away,' said Gajli. 'Let's ask my friend Magru for help. He's an estuarine crocodile—the largest crocodile in the world—and he swims really well.'

Magru immediately agreed to help. Kiku was happy to hop onto his back, while Gajli swam alongside and Woka flew over them.

They were moving along, looking for the island, when Magru suddenly shouted, 'Ouch, ouch, ouch!'

'What happened? Are you okay?' asked Woka worriedly.

'Oh, I think my leg is caught in a fishing net,' cried Magru.

'Fishing net? What are fishing nets doing here?' Woka wondered out loud.

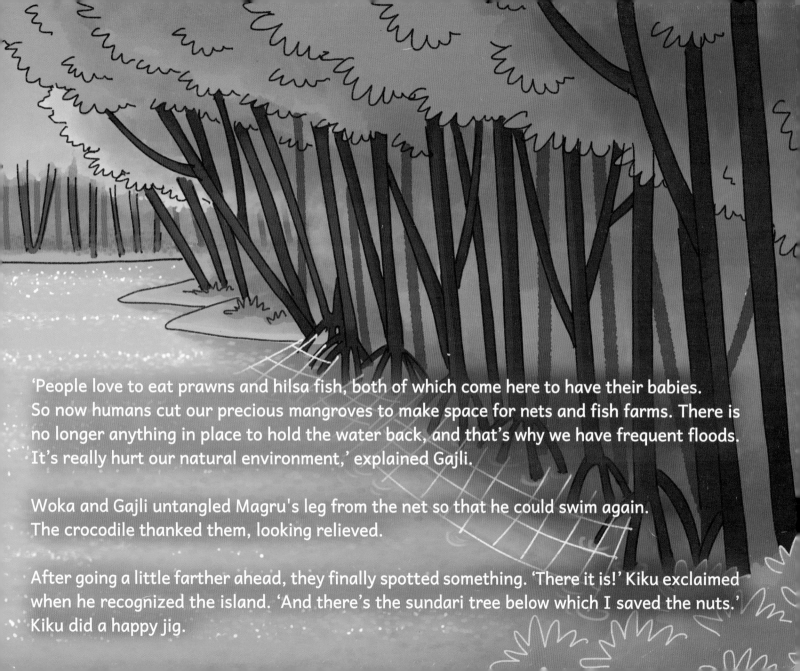

'People love to eat prawns and hilsa fish, both of which come here to have their babies. So now humans cut our precious mangroves to make space for nets and fish farms. There is no longer anything in place to hold the water back, and that's why we have frequent floods. It's really hurt our natural environment,' explained Gajli.

Woka and Gajli untangled Magru's leg from the net so that he could swim again. The crocodile thanked them, looking relieved.

After going a little farther ahead, they finally spotted something. 'There it is!' Kiku exclaimed when he recognized the island. 'And there's the sundari tree below which I saved the nuts.' Kiku did a happy jig.

But he suddenly stopped
and looked upset.
'Oh, no! How do I carry
them back home?
I don't have much time to
make the necklace.'

'Why, that's what
my backpack is for!
Let's put them in here,'
said Woka.

'Don't worry, dear Kiku.
We'll help you get everything ready
for the party,' said Magru.

In just a few hours, Woka, Magru, Gajli and Kiku were back at Kiku's home. Kiku crafted a very pretty necklace for his mamma using the sundari nuts. All the friends decorated the party venue with colourful *genwa*, *kankara* and *khalsi* flowers they had collected from the forest.

They gathered delicious fruits and nuts, and prepared little cups of honey for the guests.

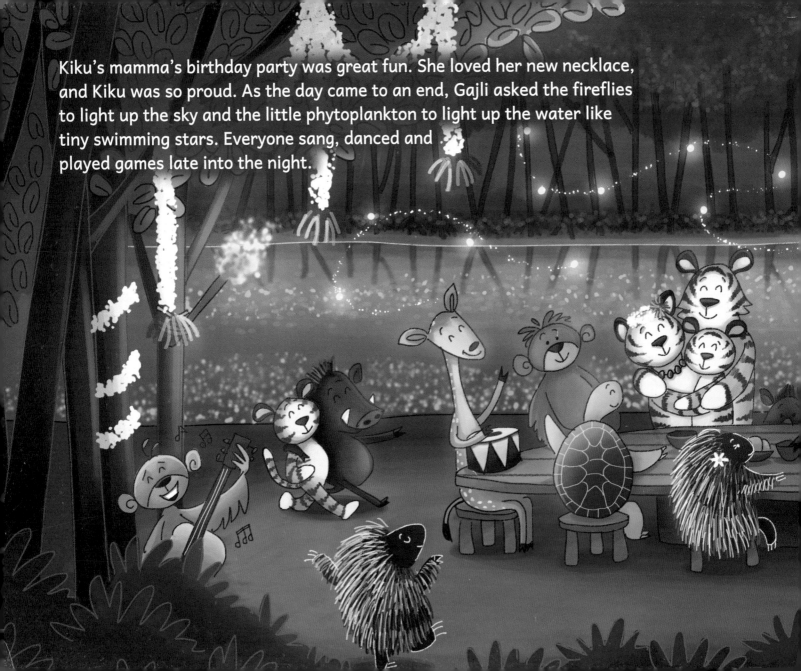

Kiku's mamma's birthday party was great fun. She loved her new necklace, and Kiku was so proud. As the day came to an end, Gajli asked the fireflies to light up the sky and the little phytoplankton to light up the water like tiny swimming stars. Everyone sang, danced and played games late into the night.

After the party, Woka declared that it was time for her to return home.
She gave all her new friends a big hug; Kiku got a special long one.
She promised to stay in touch and asked trusty GeePee to lead her back to Mumbai.

Back home, Woka cozily settled into her favourite chair. Sipping some delicious masala chai, she fondly looked at photos of her new friends on her laptop, dreamily wondering where her next adventure would take her.

Facts about the Sunderbans

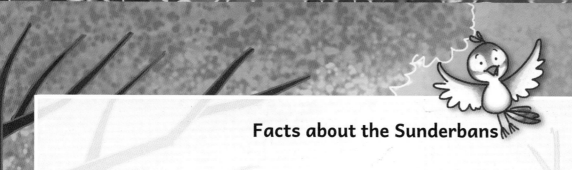

1. The Sunderbans is the world's largest coastal mangrove forest and is spread between India and our neighbouring country Bangladesh.

2. It is considered one of the natural wonders of the world and is a UNESCO World Heritage Site.

3. The Sunderbans consists of over 100 small islands. It is almost entirely covered by a dense network of river channels, estuaries and creeks, making boats the main mode of transportation from one island to the other.

4. It is home to the majestic Bengal tiger and is known to have the largest tiger population in the entire world.

5. The Sunderbans is one of the most plentiful mangrove forests in the world, with hundreds of species of birds, mammals, reptiles, fish and plants. But harmful actions by some people, like too much fishing, polluting the water and hunting, put the Sunderbans in danger.

Birthdays are fun!
How would you celebrate your
mother's or father's birthday?

I love helping others.
Have you ever helped a friend
who was sad? How?

WOKA
goes to
PANGONG
LAKE

TING TONG!!

'*Sa re ga ma*,' sang Woka one
morning as she dusted the furniture
in her house. She spotted her favourite book,
My Beautiful India, and sat down with it. Just then the doorbell rang.
It was Woka's best friend, Coppy, a pretty coppersmith barbet, Mumbai's official bird.

They flipped through the book till they came upon a magnificent page. 'Pangong Lake is the largest saltwater lake in Asia and is situated in the cold desert of Ladakh,' Coppy read out loud.

'Wow, this is where I'll go! Look, I'll even get to see the Khardung La pass,the highest motorable road in the world,' Woka declared.

She packed her bag, put on her woolly cap and scarf and punched her destination into GeePee, her assistant. 'GeePee, how long will it take to reach Pangong Lake?'

'*2 nights and 3 days*,' flashed GeePee's screen.

'Wow, that's one long trip.
Best to get started right away.'
And with that, away she flew.

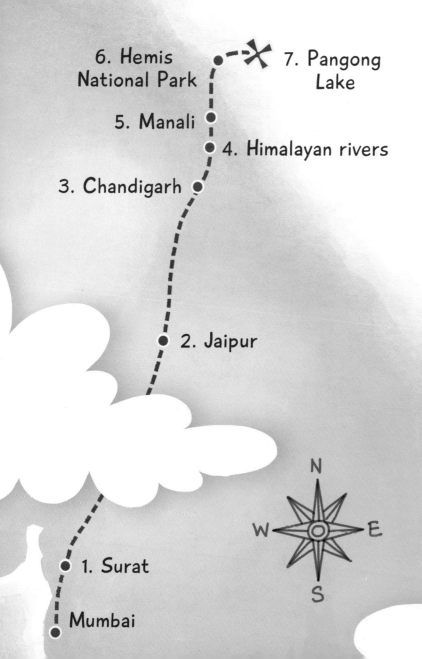

6. Hemis National Park

7. Pangong Lake

5. Manali

4. Himalayan rivers

3. Chandigarh

2. Jaipur

1. Surat

Mumbai

N
W   E
S

She soared over Surat,
the city of diamonds,
and spent the first night at the
Jantar Mantar in Jaipur.

She flew non-stop on the second
day and slept in Chandigarh's
famous Rock Garden that night.

On the third day, she flew over
noisy Himalayan rivers and ate
a delicious fresh apple in Manali,
then flew past Hemis National
Park, where she spotted a cute
snow leopard cub hiding behind
a tree.

Finally, late that night
she reached beautiful Pangong Lake,
known as Pangong Tso in Ladakhi,
the local language. Woka was so
tired after her long journey that
she fell asleep right away.

1. Surat

2. Jaipur

3. Chandigarh

4. Himalayan rivers

5. Manali

6. Hemis National Park

7. Pangong Lake

The next morning, Woka awoke to majestic golden mountains, a beautiful blue sky with pillow-soft clouds and the magical multicoloured water of Pangong Tso shimmering in the Himalayan sun. Gulls flew overhead and Brahminy ducks swam serenely in the lake.

'My India is really so gorgeous,' she said with a sigh.
'It's time to start exploring this magical place.'

'Tee-hee-hee,' giggled Woka as she dipped her feet into the icy water of the lake. A paddling of ducks came up to her. '*Juley*,' they said in unison.

'July? It's April,' replied Woka.

'Juley means "hello" in our Ladakhi,' laughed the tallest duck.'I am BrimBram and this is my family. What's your name, little sparrow?'

'Oh, juley, juley!' said Woka, who loved making new friends. 'I'm Woka Chimni and I'm from Mumbai.'

Woka flew around, admiring the scenery, when suddenly, she heard loud whistles. As she flew towards the sound, she noticed a small crowd of little bear-like creatures with chocolate-brown coats. 'Oh, these are marmots! Their whistles mean they are worried. I must find out why.'

She flew down to them. 'Juley! My name is Woka Chimni. Is everything all right?'

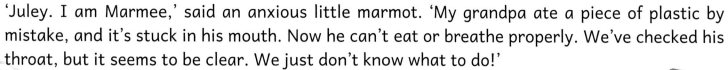

'Juley. I am Marmee,' said an anxious little marmot. 'My grandpa ate a piece of plastic by mistake, and it's stuck in his mouth. Now he can't eat or breathe properly. We've checked his throat, but it seems to be clear. We just don't know what to do!'

'May I take a look?' offered Woka. 'I am quite good with helping sick animals. My friends often call me Doc Wok.'

'Please do!' said all the marmots in unison.

Woka came close to Grandpa and gently patted his face with her wing. 'Grandpa, could you please open your mouth?'

Woka peered down his throat using GeePee's inbuilt torch. It did look all clear. Just as she was about to say something to Grandpa, she noticed something shining on the roof of his mouth.

'The wrapper is stuck to the top. No wonder none of you could spot it! I can easily remove it.' Woka reached into Grandpa's mouth and carefully took out the piece of plastic.

Grandpa spluttered and coughed, but then smiled. 'Phew! I feel so much better now. Thank you,' he said. All the marmots clapped for Woka, and little Marmee gave her a big hug.

But Woka was puzzled. 'Why is there so much plastic in this beautiful place anyway?'

Oh, thousands of people come to Pangong each year to admire its beauty and take pictures. But they throw all their plastic waste everywhere. It's spoiling our lovely home,' said Grandpa. 'Sadly, so many lovely birds and animals have disappeared from Ladakh. Even the chirus and urials have stopped coming here,' said BrimBram, joining the group.

CLEANLINESS LEVEL: VERY POOR
GROUND QUALITY: VERY POOR
WATER QUALITY: POOR
OVERALL SCORE: 30

Seeing Woka's confused expression, he continued, 'Chirus are Tibetan antelopes and urials are the wild red sheep who used to roam this region.'

Woka could not believe it. She asked GeePee to scan the area with its special lens. GeePee quickly reported, 'Cleanliness level: very poor; ground quality: very poor; water quality: poor. Overall score: 30 on 100.'

'Oh, no, this is dangerous!
We should clean up Pangong Lake,' declared Woka.

The marmots agreed but knew they needed more help.
'We will ask all the gulls, magpies and redstarts to
spread the message,' suggested Marmee.

Soon, animals and birds from the neighbouring
lakes of Tso Kar and Tso Moriri arrived.

Even an argali, the largest sheep
in the world, turned up to
help. Joining him were a
bharal—a blue sheep—and
a kiang, the largest wild
donkey in the world.

Woka used GeePee's microphone setting to give everyone instructions for the big clean-up. The gulls and ducks took charge of cleaning the lake, while the sheep and donkeys started picking up the wrappers, straws and plastic bottles strewn everywhere.

And the little marmots? Well, they made a long chain and piled up all the rubbish in a spot in the centre. A garbage truck would collect it from here the next day.

GeePee scanned the area with its special lens one more time. This time its screen flashed: *'Very clean. Overall score: 100 on 100.'*

In the evening, just as the creatures sat down together, they heard the clip-clop sound of hooves. Who could it be?

They all gasped when they saw hundreds of chirus and urials coming towards them!

'We heard that you cleaned up Pangong Tso,' the leader of the Chirus said with a warm smile. 'Pangong is one of our favourite spots, but all that garbage made it unsafe for us. Not any more, though.'

Seeing the chirus and urials was cause for great celebration. Everyone sang songs and shared stories with Woka late into the evening. Sounds of chants from the monastery nearby drifted towards them, and all the animals gathered around Woka to thank her for her help.

'I had an amazing time too,' said Woka as she looked up at the sky. Thousands of stars glittered above the magical waters of Pangong Tso. 'But it's time for me to return home.'

Three days later, Woka was back in Mumbai. Coppy and she sat on the branch outside her home, watching the sunset and enjoying their masala chai. Woka told Coppy all about her memorable trip and the amazing sight of the chirus and urials returning to Pangong. Coppy put his wing around Woka. 'I can't wait to find out where your next adventure will be.'

Facts about Pangong Lake

1. Pangong Lake is situated in the Ladakh region of Jammu and Kashmir. Since Ladakh is a cold desert, it never rains here.

2. It is the world's highest saltwater lake. Salt water usually freezes at a much lower temperature than fresh water. But, despite having only salt water, Pangong Lake freezes over in the winter.

3. Pangong is an 'endorheic' lake, which means it is totally landlocked and doesn't let water flow to other water bodies.

4. Ladakh is home to over 225 species of birds, and Pangong acts as a breeding ground (a perfect place to lay eggs) for many native and migratory birds.

5. The animals of Ladakh include yaks, sheep, wild goats, donkeys, marmots, antelopes and the endangered snow leopard.

6. The hunting of chirus (Tibetan antelopes) for their soft wool, which is used to make shahtoosh shawls, has led to the species becoming endangered.

7. The beautiful environment of Pangong Lake is threatened by those tourists who don't care about their actions and leave behind plastic bottles, wrappers and trash.

8. Animals like marmots are badly affected when they are fed biscuits or other food not meant for them.

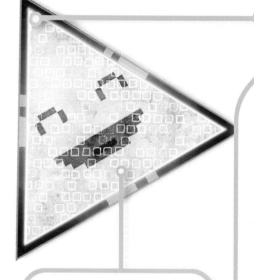

CAN YOU GUESS THE NAMES OF THE PLACES THAT WOKA FLEW OVER BY LOOKING AT THESE CLUES?

Raipur   Hemis National Park   Chandigarh

Himalayan rivers   Nagpur   Nashik

I hope you enjoyed the story of my trip to the Sunderbans and to Pangong Lake. Look out for the next book in my series of adventures exploring our beautiful India!

Other books from FunOKPlease

About FunOKPlease

We publish books for the curious little Indian! Our books aim to help kids develop an understanding of the world around them and learn important educational concepts and life skills, all in a context that is distinctly modern and Indian. We also create customized books for schools and organizations for their private circulation. For more information, please visit us at www.funokplease.com

Write to the author at preeti@funokplease.com

 facebook.com/funokplease   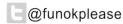 @funokplease

To my darling Neel,
Hopefully some day my love for nature
will be as pure as yours.